Mrs. Long

		DATE DUE		

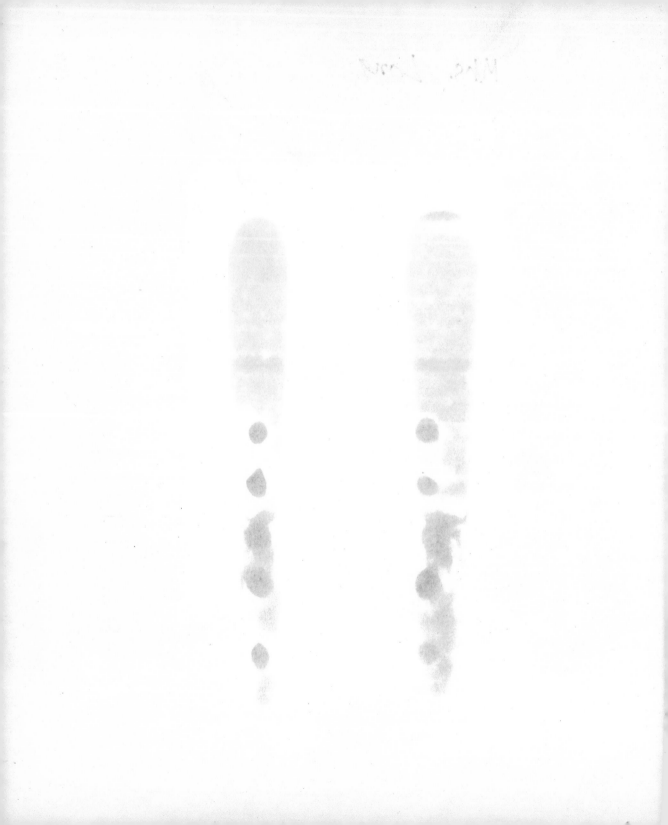

WHEAT

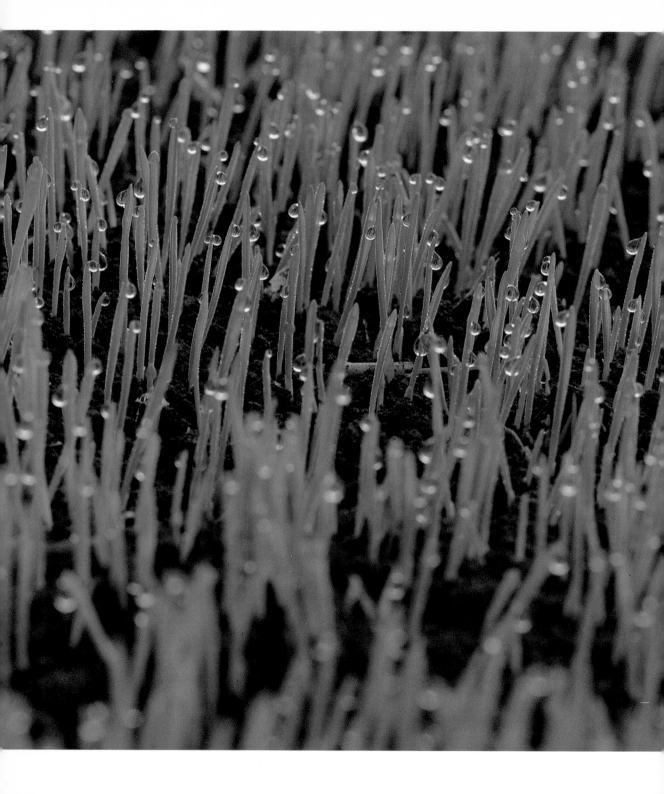

WHEAT

by Sylvia A. Johnson

Photographs by Masaharu Suzuki

A Lerner Natural Science Book

Lerner Publications Company ▪ Minneapolis

Sylvia A. Johnson, Series Editor

Translation of original text by Wesley M. Jacobsen

The publisher wishes to thank Robert Busch, Research Geneticist, Agricultural Research Service, U. S. Department of Agriculture, for his assistance in the preparation of this book.

Additional photographs by: p. 10, Jerry Bushey; p. 16, U. S. Department of Agriculture; p. 40, John Deere Company; pp. 41, 43, 44, Harvest States Cooperatives, St. Paul, Minnesota

The glossary on page 45 gives definitions and pronunciations of words shown in **bold type** in the text.

LIBRARY OF CONGRESS CATALOGING-IN-PUBLICATION DATA

Johnson, Sylvia A.
  Wheat / by Sylvia A. Johnson: photographs by Masaharu Suzuki: [translation of original text by Wesley M. Jacobsen].
    p.   cm. — (A Lerner natural science book)
  Adaptation of: Mugi no isshō / Masaharu Suzuki.
  Summary: Explains the life cycle of wheat, its varieties, its cultivation, its harvesting, and its importance in feeding millions of people all over the world.
  ISBN 0-8225-1490-7 (lib. bdg.)
  1. Wheat — Juvenile literature. [1. Wheat.]
I. Suzuki, Masaharu, ill. II. Suzuki, Masaharu. Mugi no isshō. III. Title. IV. Series.
SB191.W5J59   1990   89-13237
633.1'1 — dc20   CIP
                                            AC

International Standard Book Number: 0-8225-1490-7
Library of Congress Catalog Number: 89-13237

1 2 3 4 5 6 7 8 9 10 99 98 97 96 95 94 93 92 91 90

The wind ripples through a field of ripe wheat like waves rolling over the ocean.

"Oh beautiful for spacious skies, for amber waves of grain." These words from the song "America the Beautiful" describe a common sight on the plains of the United States and Canada—a field of ripe wheat swaying gently in the wind.

North America is not the only continent that produces this precious amber grain. More acres of land on the earth's surface are devoted to growing wheat than to the production of any other food crop. Wheat is the world's most important grain, providing food for millions of people daily.

A wheat field in early summer. The nourishing wheat grains are developing in the heads at the tops of the plant stems.

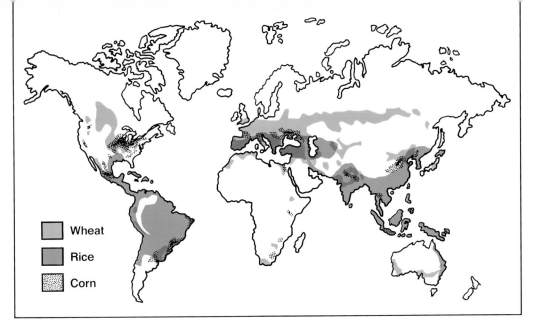

Areas where wheat, rice, and corn are grown

NOURISHING GRAINS

Like rice and corn, two other major food crops, wheat is a member of the grass family. As a part of their life cycles, these cultivated grasses produce small kernels called **grains**. Grains of wheat, rice, and corn are filled with nutrients. Wheat grains are usually ground into flour that is used to make bread, pasta, and other food products. Grains of rice and corn are eaten as food or processed to make many different kinds of products.

In North America, corn and wheat are the most important grain crops. They are planted in fields that stretch for miles across the central part of the continent. Wheat is also an important crop in Europe and northern Asia. In the southern part of Asia and in other areas where the climate is hot and wet, rice is the leading grain.

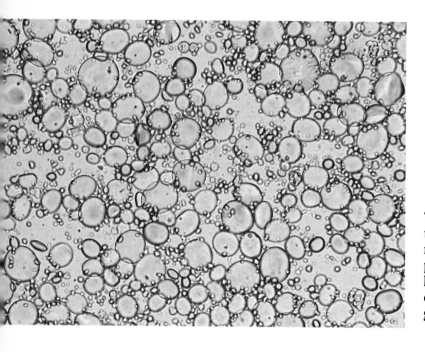

This photograph taken through a microscope shows particles of carbohydrates within the endosperm of a grain of wheat.

Why is a tiny grain of wheat such a good source of food energy? The answer to this question is easier to understand if you know what role the grain plays in the life of the wheat plant.

A grain of wheat contains the **seed** of a wheat plant, surrounded by a protective covering. It includes all the material from which a new plant can grow. Part of this material is a tiny **embryo** or **germ**, which is the beginning of the new plant. Most of the seed is made up of a substance called **endosperm**, which can nourish a growing plant.

Endosperm is a storehouse of carbohydrates and other kinds of nutrients. It is this stored food in the grain that makes wheat products like bread and noodles such a nourishing part of the human diet.

8

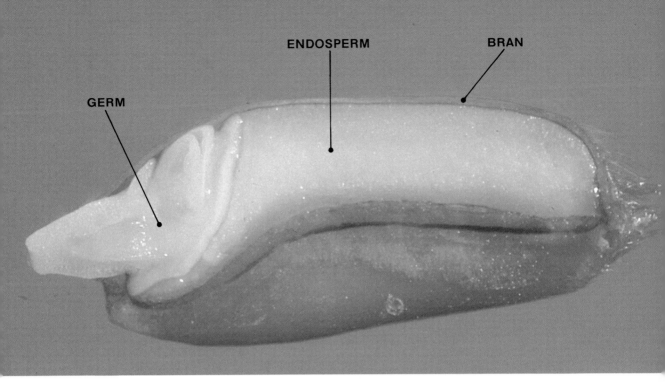

GERM · ENDOSPERM · BRAN

The *germ* of a wheat grain includes a tiny root and shoot that can develop into a new plant. Most of the grain is made up of nourishing *endosperm.* On the outside is a protective covering called the *bran.*

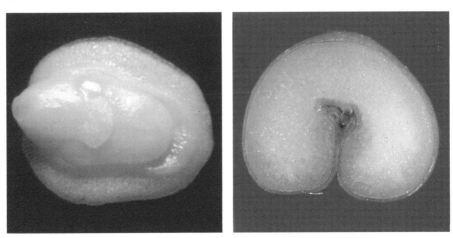

Left: The germ or embryo as it looks when removed from the grain. *Right:* This view of a wheat grain cut sideways shows the deep groove that runs the length of the grain. The groove can also been seen in the photograph above.

Farmers in North America usually plant wheat with a piece of equipment called a grain drill. Pulled by a tractor, the drill cuts a series of furrows in the ground and drops in the seeds one at a time. Another part of the machine covers the seeds with soil.

PLANTING THE SEEDS

The process that produces bread and other wheat products begins when farmers put the wheat seeds into the ground. Planting takes place at different times of year, depending on the kind of wheat being grown and the climate of the region.

There are two major kinds of wheat grown throughout the world. One kind is called **winter wheat,** and the other is known as **spring wheat.** In order to produce grain, winter wheat needs to live through a period of cold weather. Spring wheat cannot survive the cold. This kind of wheat needs a long, uninterrupted season of warm weather in order to grow.

10

In many parts of the world, winter wheat is the most common kind. In areas like the central and southern United States, China, Japan, and most of the countries of Europe, wheat seeds are planted and begin to develop in the autumn. During the winter, the young plants rest, often covered by a blanket of snow. When the weather becomes warmer, they continue their development, and by late spring, they are ready for harvest.

Spring wheat is most frequently grown in places like Canada, the northern United States, and parts of the Soviet Union, where winters are very cold. The seeds are planted in the spring and develop during the summer. Harvesting takes place from mid-summer to autumn.

Areas in North America where winter and spring wheat are grown

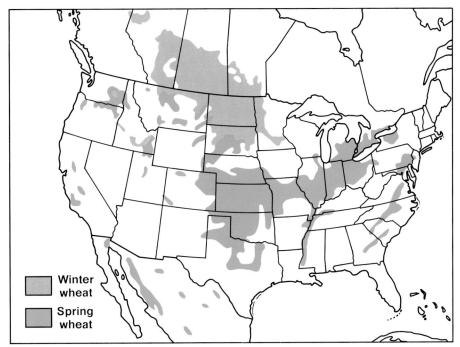

Winter wheat

Spring wheat

Above left: Two days after planting, the covering of the seed begins to split. *Above right:* Four days after planting, the shoot and root begin to develop. *Right:* Six days after planting, fine hairs have appeared on the roots. The shoot, hidden under a protective covering, is ready to emerge from the earth.

THE WHEAT BEGINS TO GROW

Whether it is planted in autumn or spring, wheat goes through the same kind of early development. Buried in moist soil, the seed begins to sprout as the growing embryo breaks through the seed covering. Soon a slender white **shoot** appears; this will become the plant's stem and first leaf. At the same time, fine roots begin to reach down into the soil.

The shoot of a wheat plant is covered by a kind of cap that scientists call a **coleoptile**. This structure is also known as a sheath leaf, but it is not a true leaf. The coleoptile protects the tiny shoot as it pushes its way up through the soil. Soon after the coleoptile emerges into the light, the first true leaves begin their development.

12

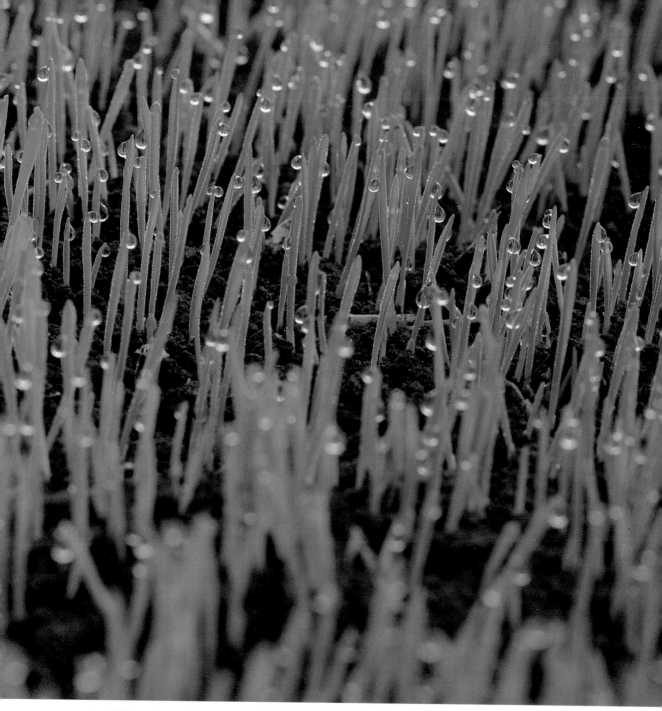

Like tiny spears, the coleoptiles of young wheat plants point toward the sky. In this photograph, the true leaves have just started to break through the coleoptiles.

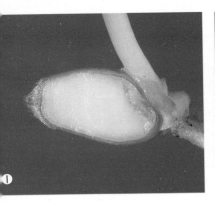

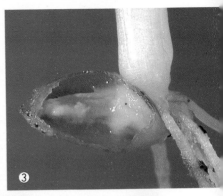

These photographs show how the endosperm in the seed is gradually used up as the young plant develops. (1) The endosperm around the time that the coleoptile emerges from the soil. It has a milky look because it has absorbed water. (2) By the time that the second true leaf appears, the endosperm has started to decrease. (3) The endosperm is almost gone by the time that the third leaf develops. (4) When the seed becomes shriveled and dry, the leaves begin to supply food for the growing plant.

During this early period of growth, the wheat plant is nourished by the endosperm stored in the seed. This substance provides all the energy needed for the development of the young stem, root, and leaves.

As the milky endosperm is used up, the seed gradually shrinks. By the time that several of the true leaves have emerged, it is dry and shriveled. The seed's role in the life of the wheat plant is finished. Now it is time for the leaves to take over the job of supplying energy for the plant's growth.

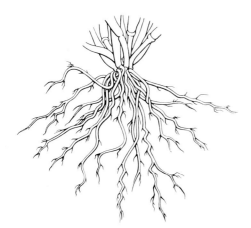

While the wheat leaves develop above the ground, roots are growing below. Wheat, like all grass plants, has a *fibrous root system.* Instead of one main root, or tap root, with smaller secondary roots growing from it, a grass root system is made up of many slender roots that are similar in size (left).

Each small root (right) has a delicate tip that is protected by a group of cells known as the *root cap.* Above the tip is an area covered with fine hairs. These *root hairs* absorb water and minerals from the soil.

A cross-section of a wheat root. The round cells in the outer section store nutrients and water. In the core of the root are tube-shaped cells that are part of the plant's transportation system.

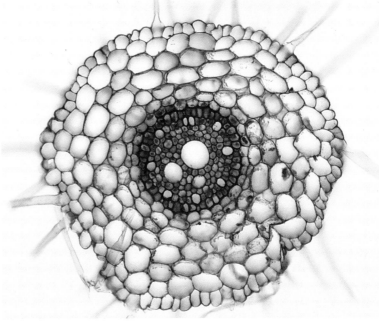

15

A field of young wheat. Using energy from the sun, the green leaves produce the food needed for growth.

FOOD FACTORIES IN THE LEAVES

The leaves of a wheat plant look very different from the leaves of many other kinds of green plants. Like all members of the grass family, wheat has long, narrow leaves made up of two parts, a **sheath** and a **blade**. The sheath is the lower part of the leaf, and it grows wrapped around the plant stem. The flat, pointed blade is connected to the top of the sheath.

16

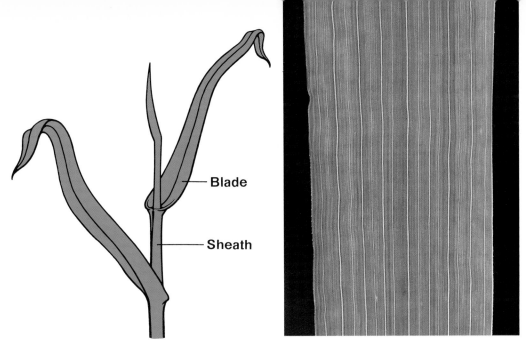

The blade and sheath of a wheat leaf (left) have long parallel rows of veins (right). This system of veins, found in all grasses, is very different from the net-like veins in the leaves of other plants.

These long, narrow leaves play a very important role in the life of the wheat plant. They help to produce nutrients needed for continued growth. The nutrients are manufactured through a complicated process called **photosynthesis**. Photosynthesis means "putting together with light," and this is exactly what the leaves do. They produce food by using the energy of the sun to combine raw materials drawn from the air and the soil.

From the air, the leaves take carbon dioxide, a gas given off by living things during the process of respiration. Carbon dioxide enters into the plants through tiny openings on the leaves called **stomata**. Water, the other essential material for photosynthesis, is drawn from the soil through the roots.

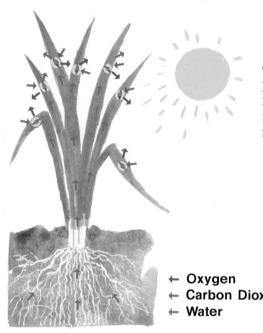

Carbon dioxide and water provide the raw materials for photosynthesis. Oxygen is a byproduct of this food-making process.

← Oxygen
← Carbon Dioxide
← Water

Photosynthesis takes place in the cells of the plant's leaves. Within these cells are tiny bodies called **chloroplasts**, which contain the green pigment **chlorophyll**. Chlorophyll is the material that gives plants their green color, and it also plays a vital role in the food-making process.

By absorbing sunlight, chlorophyll produces the energy that breaks down and then combines the molecules of water and carbon dioxide. The results of this synthesis are two new substances—oxygen and a form of sugar known as **glucose**.

Glucose is the basic food used by a plant in growing, reproducing, and carrying on all of its life processes. The plant also uses some oxygen, but most of this gas is released through the stomata into the atmosphere. Here it supplies the essential element for the respiration of all forms of animal life, including human beings.

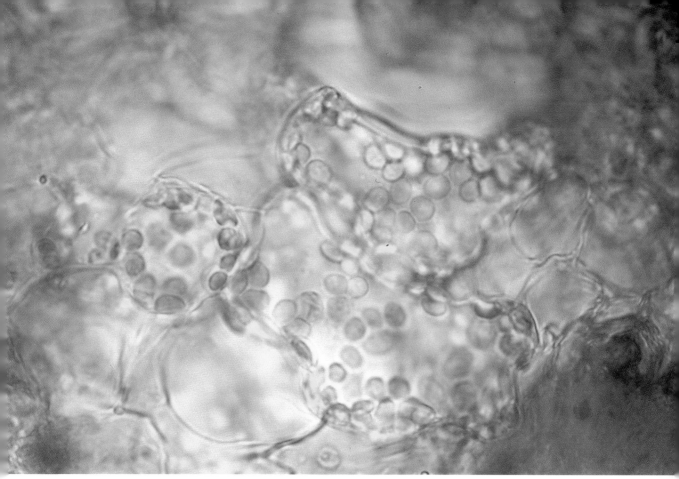

Above: This greatly magnified photograph shows the chloroplasts in the cells of a wheat plant's leaf. The tiny bodies contain the green pigment chlorophyll.

Right: The openings, or stomata, in a wheat leaf are arranged in rows parallel to the center vein. Carbon dioxide is taken into the leaf through these openings, and oxygen is released.

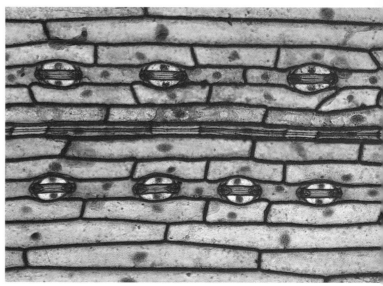

This wheat plant has been cut vertically so that you can see the new stems, or tillers, that have developed from the original stem.

TILLERING: GROWING NEW STEMS

All green plants use food created through photosynthesis to grow new leaves and thicker, longer roots and stems. Wheat and other plants in the grass family also use this energy to grow in another way. They produce whole new stems.

At the base of a wheat plant's original stem are special points known as **nodes**. It is from these points that new stems develop. They grow right next to the original stem, remaining attached to it and to the plant's root system. Wheat plants that are not crowded together can produce around 15 stems, each with its own leaves.

These new stems are called **tillers**, and the method of growth that produces them is known as **tillering**. It is common to many members of the grass family, including wheat, rice, and varieties of wild grasses.

A plant cut horizontally reveals the original stem (1) and the tillers growing from it. The numbers indicate the order in which the tillers appeared. The red arrows point to tillers that are offshoots of other tillers.

Opposite: Young winter wheat plants coated with frost. As winter approaches, the plants will enter a period of dormancy. *Right:* During the coldest part of the winter, the wheat plants rest, protected by a blanket of snow.

WINTER WHEAT: LIVING THROUGH THE COLD

Wheat planted in the autumn has a few months to grow before cold weather comes. The young plants produce roots, leaves, and tillers and become well established in the soil. Then the falling temperature halts their development.

During the coldest part of the winter, the wheat goes into a resting state called **dormancy.** Photosynthesis does not take place, and the plants live on stored food. The wheat does not grow during this period, but it is getting ready for the season of growth that is to come.

If it is not exposed to cold temperatures, winter wheat will not be able to produce grain in the spring. The amount of cold weather needed depends on the variety of wheat being grown.

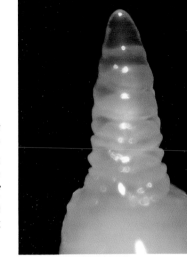

After going through the necessary period of cold weather, winter wheat begins to grow again, even though winter may still linger (opposite). During this period of development, tiny heads begin to grow inside the tips of the plant stems (right).

Some kinds of wheat require only about four weeks of below-freezing temperatures in order to produce grain. These varieties are grown in regions like the southern part of the United States, where winters are short. Other kinds of winter wheat have to be exposed to several months of cold weather. Areas with longer winters are suitable for planting these varieties.

As soon as winter wheat plants have gone through the necessary period of cold, they begin to grow again, even though the weather may still be fairly cool. They put out new tillers, and their roots push deeper into the ground. At this stage, the plants also begin to prepare for a new kind of growth. At the tips of the stems, tiny **heads** start to develop. It is from these parts of the plants that the wheat grains will eventually grow.

While winter wheat (opposite) needs a period of cold weather in order to develop, spring wheat cannot survive winter's low temperatures.

SPRING WHEAT: GROWING WITHOUT PAUSE

Spring wheat does not need a period of cold in order to develop. From the time that the seeds are put into the ground until the plants are harvested, this kind of wheat goes through a continuous process of growth.

In the cold regions where it is raised, spring wheat is not planted until winter is completely over. The mild spring weather and the warm soil provide ideal conditions for the sprouting of seeds. Once the young plants have appeared, they grow steadily, producing leaves, tillers, and roots. By early summer, tiny heads have begun to develop at the tips of their stems.

In some parts of the world, spring wheat is not planted in the spring. Like winter wheat, it is planted in autumn. Unlike winter wheat, however, it continues to grow uninterrupted through the winter months. Harvesting takes place in late winter or early spring. This is possible in areas with very mild winters like Arizona and southern California. Spring wheat varieties are used in such regions because the winter temperatures are not cold enough for the development of winter wheat.

Still hidden within the tips of the wheat stems, the heads develop quickly in the warm spring weather. In about one month's time, they grow from 1 millimeter to 10 millimeters in length (left to right).

A NEW STAGE OF DEVELOPMENT

When winter wheat begins to grow again in spring, it grows quickly. Warmed and nourished by the spring sun, the plants add many new leaves and tillers. Then, after several weeks of rapid growth, they enter another stage of development. The plants are ready to begin the reproductive period of their lives.

At this time, the wheat plants stop producing leaves and tillers. Instead, the individual stems become taller, shooting up toward the sky. At their tips, the tiny heads are growing rapidly. They are still hidden within the stems, but soon they will emerge into the open.

In spring, winter wheat plants develop rapidly, adding many new leaves and tillers. This photograph shows wheat growing next to a field of flowering rape, a crop plant in the mustard family.

After they have completed their development, the wheat heads push their way out of the tips of the stems. They emerge between the blade and the sheath of the topmost leaf.

A wheat head gradually emerging over a period of two days. This variety of wheat has long hairs called *beards* growing on the head. Other kinds of wheat are beardless.

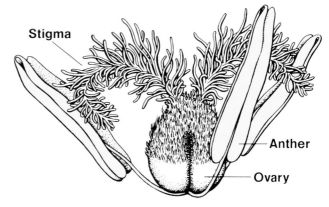

Protective scales (above) enclose the reproductive parts of a wheat flower (right).

The head of a wheat plant is actually a collection of tiny flowers. A typical wheat head is made up of about 40 to 60 flowers growing in a tight cluster. These flowers play an essential role in the process by which the plant reproduces itself. Like most other kinds of green plants, wheat reproduces sexually. Within each flower are male and female reproductive organs.

Instead of having colorful petals like roses and other garden flowers, a wheat flower is enclosed by two protective scales. The drawing on this page shows a flower with these scales removed so that you can see the reproductive parts inside.

The three long **stamens** with the enlarged **anthers** at their tips are the male parts of the flower. They produce **pollen** that contains male reproductive cells, or **sperm**. The two hairy **stigmas** are connected by stalk-like **styles** to a chamber known as the **ovary**. Together these three parts form the **pistil**, the flower's female organ. Within the ovary is a tiny structure called an **ovule**, which contains a female egg cell.

31

Stages in the pollination of a wheat flower. (1) The scales open. (2) The stamens emerge and release pollen. (3) The pollen becomes attached to the hairy stigmas hidden deep in the flower. (4) The scales close. The whole process takes about 30 minutes.

POLLINATION

Several days after the heads emerge, the wheat flowers are ready to bloom. The protective scales open for a short time, exposing the anthers and the stigmas. In order for reproduction to take place, pollen produced by the anthers must first be transferred to the stigmas. This transfer is called **pollination**.

Roses and many other flowering plants are pollinated by insects that are looking for nectar or pollen. Plants in the grass family depend on the wind to carry pollen from the anthers to the stigmas.

When wheat is pollinated, pollen usually drifts from the anthers to the stigmas of the same flower or of another flower on the same plant. Scientists call this **self-pollination.** In many wild grasses, as well as some cultivated ones like rye, the pollen from one flower is carried to the stigmas of a flower on another plant. This is known as **cross-pollination**.

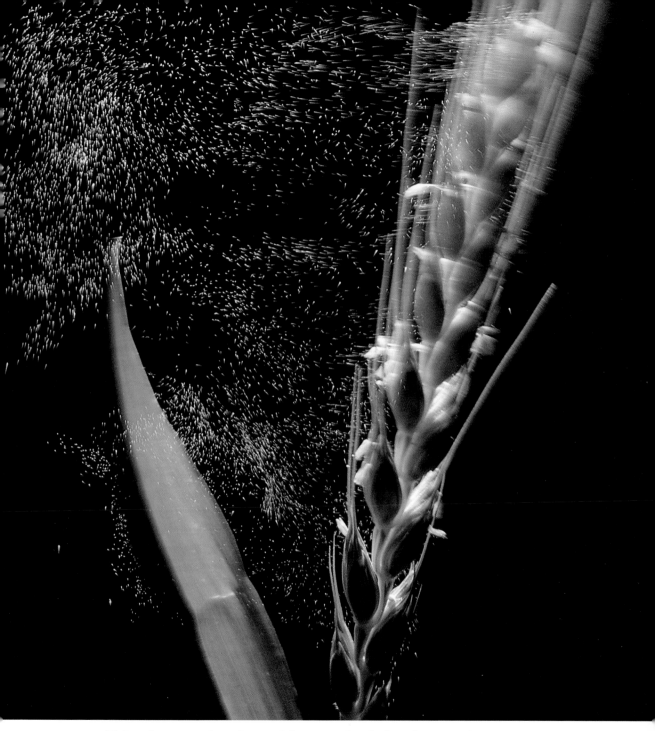

This photograph taken with a strobe light shows wheat pollen drifting on a gentle May breeze.

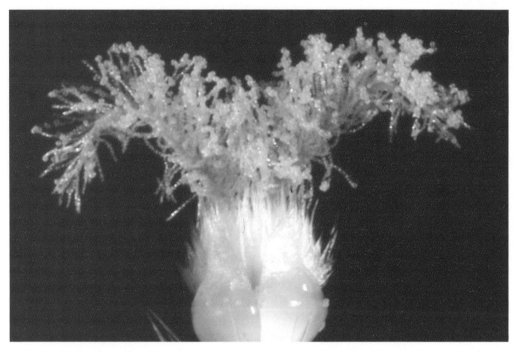

Grains of pollen clinging to the hairy stigmas of a wheat flower. The stigmas are connected by the stalk-like styles to the bulging ovary. Inside the ovary is an ovule containing a female egg cell.

FERTILIZATION

After the flowers have been pollinated, it is time for the next stage in the wheat plant's reproductive cycle, **fertilization.** This stage begins when the tiny grains of pollen on the stigmas split and send out tubes that extend down the styles into the ovary. Sperm move down through the tiny tubes. Eventually one sperm unites with the egg cell within the ovule. The egg cell is now fertilized, and a wheat seed begins to grow.

34

Right: A magnified photograph of pollen grains. *Below:* This remarkable photo shows the tiny tubes that develop from the pollen grains. The tubes pass through the fine hairs on the stigmas, into the styles, and finally down into the ovary. Through these tubes, sperm enter the ovary. When one sperm unites with the egg cell in the ovule, fertilization takes place.

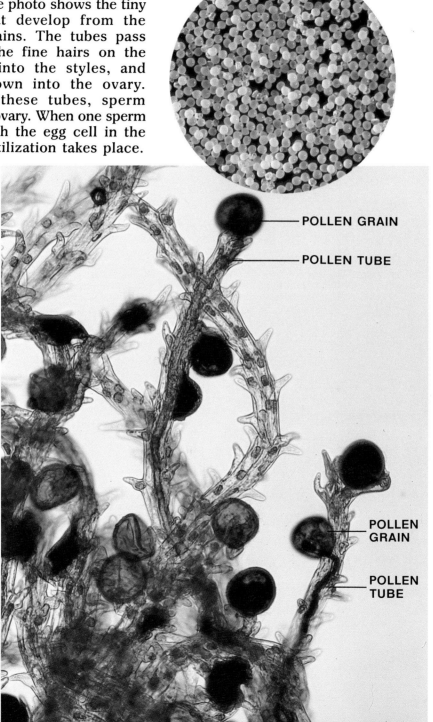

POLLEN GRAIN

POLLEN TUBE

POLLEN GRAIN

POLLEN TUBE

After pollination and fertilization, the ovary of the flower is gradually transformed into the grain, or fruit, of the wheat plant. As the seed develops inside it, the ovary enlarges and lengthens (top and middle). About one month after fertilization, the seed and the covering surrounding it begin to dry out (bottom). Soon the grain will be ready for harvest.

The seed, made up of embryo and endosperm, develops from the ovule. Surrounding the seed is the ovary, which now becomes the grain of the wheat plant. The wall of the ovary joins with the seed coat and the outermost layer of the endosperm to form the bran that covers the grain.

Botanists, scientists who study plants, refer to a grain of wheat or rice as a **fruit**. These dry, hard grains are very different from apples, peaches, and other juicy foods that people ordinarily think of as fruits. In botanical terms, however, a fruit is the part of a plant that develops from the ovary and that encloses the seeds. This is exactly what wheat grains are.

A field of wheat ready for harvest

After they begin to form, the wheat grains develop on the heads for about a month. During this time, they become plump and filled with endosperm. Then they gradually dry out. At this time, the leaves of the wheat plant also become dry and yellow. Their green chlorophyl is no longer needed to provide nourishment for the plant. Its cycle of growth—from seed to seed—has been completed.

HARVESTING THE WHEAT

When the heads of grain are fully developed and heavy on the stems, it is time to harvest the wheat. In order to have the most successful harvest, the wheat grains must be very dry. Their moisture content has to be below 14 percent. If damp grains of wheat are harvested and then stored, they may spoil.

The wheat crop is ready for harvest at different times throughout the world. In the southern part of North America, for example, winter wheat may be harvested as early as May. In the central section of the continent, in Kansas and Nebraska, harvesting often takes place in June. Spring wheat is not usually ready for harvest until late summer or autumn. August is harvesttime in states like Minnesota and North Dakota. In Canada, the wheat fields may not be cut until September.

Most modern farmers harvest wheat with a large machine called a **combine.** This piece of equipment was given its name because it combines two different steps involved in harvesting. These steps are reaping (cutting) and threshing, or separating the grains from the rest of the plant material.

A combine has a sharp blade on the front that cuts the wheat stems. As the machine moves across a field, rotating paddles press the plants against this blade. The cut plants are then carried by a conveyer belt into a revolving drum where the threshing process begins. Here the grain heads are beaten off the stems. The dried stems and leaves, which are now known as **straw**, are dropped out the back of the combine.

Inside the combine, the grain goes on to another stage in the threshing. It passes through a series of sieves in which it is separated from the other parts of the head, which are blown out of the combine by fans. The grain is then put into a holding tank. When the tank becomes full, the wheat

As it moves across the field, a combine cuts the wheat and separates the grain from the other parts of the plants.

A load of harvested wheat is deposited in a truck.

is dumped into a truck and hauled away for storage.

One of the things that make wheat and other grains such useful crops is their ability to be stored for long periods of time. As long as wheat grains have been thoroughly dried, they will keep indefinitely.

Most wheat is stored in tall buildings called **grain elevators**. The grain is brought by trucks or railroad cars to the elevators. Conveyor belts carry it to the tops of the structures, where it is cleaned and weighed. Then the grain is deposited in bins in the lower sections of the elevators. Here it will be stored until it is ready to be shipped to processing plants.

FROM GRAIN TO FOOD

Wheat grains can be made into all kinds of products that provide food for people and animals. Most wheat is ground into flour that is used to make bread, cakes, cookies, and crackers. Some wheat is processed to produce spaghetti, noodles, and other kinds of pasta. Many breakfast cereals are also made out of wheat.

Different types of wheat are used to make different wheat products. For example, bread flour comes from wheat that has a high percentage of **gluten** in the endosperm. Gluten is a protein that makes bread rise when yeast is added to it. **Durum** is the type of wheat most often used in producing pasta. Its hard grains can be made into pasta products that won't stick together when they are cooked.

Wheat is usually processed in giant factories called **mills**. Here the grains of wheat are first cleaned, moistened with water, and then ground by a series of heavy steel rollers. Whole wheat flour is made by grinding the entire grain, including the endosperm, germ, and bran. White flour is made from the endosperm only. The other parts of the grain are separated from the endosperm during the grinding process. Wheat germ and bran are used both as animal feed and as food for humans.

Pasta is also made by grinding wheat grains into a coarse flour. Water is then added to make a kind of paste.

In these milling machines (above), wheat grains are ground into a coarse flour (right) that will be used to make spaghetti, macaroni, and other kinds of pasta.

Pasta products like spaghetti and lasagna noodles are among the nourishing foods made from wheat.

Spaghetti, macaroni, and many of the other varieties of pasta are made by forcing the paste through machines that produce different shapes. The pasta is then dried until it becomes hard. Noodles come from wheat paste that is rolled into sheets and cut into strips.

Whether it is made into noodles, breakfast cereal, or bread, wheat is a vital part of the human diet. The tiny amber grains produced by wheat plants provide nourishment for millions of people all over the world.

GLOSSARY

anthers—the enlarged tips of the stamens, where pollen is produced

beards—the hairs that grow on the heads of some varieties of wheat

blade—the flat upper part of a grass leaf

chlorophyll (KLOR-uh-fil)—a green pigment that absorbs sunlight, producing the energy that makes photosynthesis possible

chloroplasts (KLOR-uh-plasts)—tiny bodies in plant cells that contain chlorophyll

coleoptile (ko-lee-AHP-t'l)—a sheath-like structure that protects the developing shoot of wheat and other grass plants

combine (CAHM-bine)—a machine that cuts the wheat and separates the grains from the rest of the plant

cross-pollination—the transfer of pollen from the anthers of one flower to the stigmas of a flower on another plant

dormancy (DOR-muhn-see)—a state of rest and inactivity. Winter wheat goes through a period of dormancy during the cold winter months.

durum (DUR-uhm)—a type of hard-grained wheat used to make pasta products

embryo (EM-bree-oh)—the part of a seed that will develop into a new plant; the germ

endosperm (EN-duh-sperm)—the material in a seed that provides nourishment for the embryo and young plant. The endosperm in wheat is also ground into flour to make food for humans.

fertilization—the union of a male sperm with a female egg cell

fibrous root system—a root system made up of many fine, branching roots. Wheat and other plants in the grass family have fibrous roots.

fruit—the part of a plant that develops from the ovary and encloses the seeds

germ—the part of a seed that will develop into a new plant; the embryo

glucose (GLOO-kose)—a form of sugar produced by plants during photosynthesis

gluten (GLOOT-uhn)—a protein in wheat endosperm that makes bread rise when yeast is added to it. Types of wheat with a high percentage of gluten—for example, hard red wheats—are used to make bread flour.

grain elevators—tall structures in which grain is stored after harvesting

grains—dry, one-seeded fruits in which the seed coat is fused to the wall of the ovary

heads—the parts of the wheat plant where flowers develop

mills—factories where wheat grains are ground into flour

nodes—points from which tillers grow on a grass plant. The leaves develop from other nodes located on the stems.

ovary—the chamber at the base of the pistil where seeds develop

ovule (AHV-yul)—a tiny structure in the ovary that contains a female egg cell. After fertilization, the ovule develops into a seed.

photosynthesis (fot-oh-SIN-thuh-sis)—the process by which green plants use the energy of the sun to make food

pollen—a powdery substance produced by a flower's anthers that contains sperm

pollination—the transfer of pollen from the anthers to the stigmas

root cap—a group of cells that protects the tip of a developing root

root hairs—fine hairs near the tip of a root that take in water and minerals from the soil

seed—a small structure containing the material from which a new plant can grow

self-pollination—the transfer of pollen from the anthers to the stigmas of the same flower or of another flower on the same plant

sheath—the lower part of a grass leaf, which grows wrapped around the stem

shoot—the developing stem and leaves of a plant embryo

sperm—male reproductive cells

spring wheat—a kind of wheat that does not need a period of cold in order to produce grain. Spring wheat is usually planted in spring and harvested in autumn, although in some areas with very mild winters, it is planted in autumn.

stamens (STAY-muhns)—the male reproductive organs of a flower

stigmas (STIG-muhs)—the top parts of the pistil, which receive pollen

stomata (STO-muh-tuh)—the pores or openings in a leaf through which carbon dioxide is taken in and oxygen is released. The singular form of the word is **stoma.**

straw—the dried stems and leaves of wheat and other grain plants

styles—stalks that connect the stigmas to the ovary

tillering—the process of growing by producing tillers, characteristic of many members of the grass family

tillers—secondary stems that grow from the main stem of a grass plant

winter wheat—a kind of wheat that must go through a period of cold weather in order to produce grain. Winter wheat is usually planted in autumn and harvested in spring or early summer.

INDEX